THROUGH THEIR EYES

ECHOES OF SILENCE

Edited By Lynsey Evans

First published in Great Britain in 2024 by:

Young Writers
Remus House
Coltsfoot Drive
Peterborough
PE2 9BF
Telephone: 01733 890066
Website: www.youngwriters.co.uk

All Rights Reserved
Book Design by Ashley Janson
© Copyright Contributors 2024
Softback ISBN 978-1-83565-785-0
Printed and bound in the UK by BookPrintingUK
Website: www.bookprintinguk.com
YB0597Y

FOREWORD

Since 1991, here at Young Writers we have celebrated the awesome power of creative writing, especially in young adults, where it can serve as a vital method of expressing strong (and sometimes difficult) emotions, a conduit to develop empathy, and a safe, non-judgemental place to explore one's own place in the world. With every poem we see the effort and thought that each pupil published in this book has put into their work and by creating this anthology we hope to encourage them further with the ultimate goal of sparking a life-long love of writing.

Through Their Eyes challenged young writers to open their minds and pen bold, powerful poems from the points-of-view of any person or concept they could imagine – from celebrities and politicians to animals and inanimate objects, or even just to give us a glimpse of the world as they experience it. The result is this fierce collection of poetry that by turns questions injustice, imagines the innermost thoughts of influential figures or simply has fun.

The nature of the topic means that contentious or controversial figures may have been chosen as the narrators, and as such some poems may contain views or thoughts that, although may represent those of the person being written about, by no means reflect the opinions or feelings of either the author or us here at Young Writers.

We encourage young writers to express themselves and address subjects that matter to them, which sometimes means writing about sensitive or difficult topics. If you have been affected by any issues raised in this book, details on where to find help can be found at *www.youngwriters.co.uk/info/other/contact-lines*

CONTENTS

Bryngwyn Comprehensive School, Llanelli

Millie Woods (13)	1
Levi Jones (13)	2
Ffion Jones (13)	4
Jasmine Morris (13)	5
Lexie Price (12)	6
Sophia Lloyd (13)	7
Libby Davies (13)	8
Poppy Wilson (13)	9
Dylan Montenegro-Hopkins (13)	10
Livia Marchant (12)	11
Joshua Davies (13)	12
Maisie Riley (13)	13
Marysia Turko (13)	14
Kayla Hinkin (13)	15
Aleksandra Wawrzyszuk	16
Poppy Whitehead (14)	17
Cerys Stannard (14)	18
Mikey Thomas (13)	19
Lexi Rees (13)	20
Lewis Thomas (13)	21
Dewi Morgan (13)	22
Llŷr Barrett (13)	23
Daniel Griffiths (13)	24
Alfie Hartnell (13)	25
Skye Rance-Williams (12)	26

Notley High School & Braintree Sixth Form, Braintree

Eva Taylor (12)	27
Amelie Leader (14)	28
Faith Gibson (13)	30
Thomas Ross (13)	32

Jacob Clayton (12)	34
Deniz Saribal (12)	36
Jessica Stammers (11)	38
Amy Rayfield (13)	40
Grace Clark (11)	41
Ava Cataldo (13)	42
Alice Loveard (14)	43
Millie-Rose Cunnane (12)	44
Alex Frost (12)	45
Darcy Miller (14)	46
Harry Etheridge (13)	47
Elliott Barry (12)	48
Eva Tammaro (13)	49
Erin Guilder (11)	50
Fleur Thatcher (11)	51
Emily Kemp (14)	52
Luke Garraghan (14)	53
Daniel Smith (11)	54
Jamie Smith (13)	55
Bella Browning (12)	56
Imogen Sibley (12)	57
Michelle Sarpong (11)	58
Benedict Todd (11)	59
Zack Haywood (12)	60
Harvey Green (11)	61
Lia Dicker (12)	62
Darcie Cross (12)	63
Sophie Curzon (12)	64
Jake Haley (11)	65
Logan Freemantle (11)	66
Katie Kemp (12)	67

The King John School, Thundersley

Isabella Dean (11)	68
Hollie Tidiman (14)	70
Isabel Cole (13)	72
Harry Wilson (12)	74
Suraya Siddique (13)	75
Madison Alsop (13)	76
James McGettigan (14)	78
Francesca Vigilante (16)	80
Sophie Webb (14)	82
Kate Williamson (14)	83
Dylan Rott (14)	84
Melissa Tsappis (14)	86
Kye Woodruff (12)	87
Darcy Rust (14)	88
Alina Saleemi (14)	89
Rose Snook (13)	90
Aidan Armitage (12)	92
Jessica Williamson (11)	93
Ava Dowler (14)	94
Harry Thompson (12)	95
Evie Rott (11)	96
Oluwamayowa Oguntoye (12)	98
Alfie Malby (11)	99
Max Day (14)	100
Kai Wonfor (13)	101
Anaïs Buzer (14)	102
Edward Tarbard (14)	103
Daniel Cesonis (12)	104
Felix Gilbert (13)	105
John Righa (12)	106
Emma Lodge (11)	107
Roman Smale (12)	108
Daisy Stock (11)	109
Poppy Abbott (11)	110
Ryden Smith (13)	111
Maisy-Jai Roberts (11)	112
Isaac Williams (11)	113
Keira Livemore (12)	114
Oliver Plumb (14)	115
Evan Holbrook (13)	116
Zara Futcher (12)	117
Feranmi Fagbohunka (12)	118
Hannah Walkom (13)	119
Amber Longman (12)	120
George Otton (12)	121
Henry Pearch (12)	122
Mia Bentley (14)	123
Eden Pearson-Watts (12)	124
Leonard Raymond (13)	125
Holly James (12)	126
Elliot Arthurton (11)	127
William Tutton (14)	128
Aaron Eniola (13)	129
Ellis Lyons (13)	130
Lucy Hayden (12)	131
Ava Sussex-Barnes (12)	132
Violet Siggers (12)	133
Tobey Clowes (12)	134
Kasey Curtis (12)	135
Alfie Burroughs (11)	136

THE
POEMS

I'm Just Pluto

I'm just Pluto, mocked as ninth,
Was I just made to be a comet?
Not birthed to last, nor make it far,
I was an unpainted white, now I'm rusting.

I'm just Pluto, the Achilles heel of space,
The sun's gleaming, awakening aurora
Deserves to shine on my sombre, muted face,
They count me out endlessly, time and time again.

I'm just Pluto, an abandoned tree without roots,
Spiralling uncontrollably out of the boundless
Incomprehensible labyrinth-like cobweb, I call home,
I never grew up, it's getting so old.

I'm just Pluto, a bitter, bleak, cold-blooded dwarf,
My mercurial, arrhythmical sea, flooded with a sour
Stench of tears, I got disregarded like all my potential,
The melancholy of life bruised my empty canvas to ash.

I am Pluto, always a dwarf, never a planet.

Millie Woods (13)
Bryngwyn Comprehensive School, Llanelli

A Race For Glory

Bump after bump after bump.
The old car flying down the dirt track,
Dust flying into my eyes, blocking my view,
Wheels shaking and vibrating as the engine rumbles,
In this situation, all I can feel is the wheels hitting rocks,
As the spectators scream and shout behind barriers,
Mere inches away from the mud-covered fenders,
Mud flaps shaking, flares gleaming,
Indicating my treacherous path,
Frantically pressing the accelerator,
The clutch to change gears,
The roll cage is rattling,
Exhaust, roaring with fire,
Co-driver screaming instructions, that are just a blur,
"Hard right! Flat out!"
The adrenaline in my body stinging me,
Flying over hills like a Harrier Jet,
My hands trembling,
My radio blaring into my ears,
Can I make my team proud?
My sponsors,
My fans,
My family,
Can I survive?
Can I win?

As the surface changes, so does my worry,
The snowy terrain slowing me down,
Making me even more nervous,
The cold, bare metal grasping my skin,
The uncomfortable seats, digging into my spine,
My heavy helmet, drooping my head down,
Could I beat the opposing team?
Can I win glory?

Levi Jones (13)
Bryngwyn Comprehensive School, Llanelli

Through The Eyes Of A Candle

As the lights go off and my light comes on,
I can feel the soft wax,
Piercing and painfully dripping down on my body,
I can hear my flame burning and fizzing,
I can smell my flowery scent blooming across the hall,
That's all I can taste is smoke choking me,
My mouth tastes like ashes,
I am in pain but I stand tall,
I can see nothing but my light fading away,
While I melt and burn away,
I am just a stupid candle,
And that's all I will ever be
Will someone burn my flame out
So I don't have a life of misery,
I just can't take it anymore,
I feel like I have been burnt through hell,
I just can't take it anymore,
I feel like I have been burnt through hell,
Please God let me melt,
My eyes droop down,
Goodbye world.

Ffion Jones (13)
Bryngwyn Comprehensive School, Llanelli

Reflecting For You

I show them their true reflection,
But that's not their desired complexion.
Falling tears when they stare at their body,
Please don't let me be the blame for you getting bloody.

I'm selfless, focused on others,
Revealing images that cause your suffers.
I wish this exasperating life would end,
If I disappeared, your insecurites would slowly mend.

Broken, smashed and shattered,
But I still glimmer even when I'm scattered.
Although, the internal feeling of shimmering is long gone,
I dream of going back to when it shone.

Stuck as a people pleaser,
Maybe if I wasn't, the pain would be easier.
I may be fractured, but my echo never dies,
Just like the everlasting thought making tears well in your glassy eyes.

Jasmine Morris (13)
Bryngwyn Comprehensive School, Llanelli

Through The Eyes Of A Bully

I feel like my parents are having issues
And will not make it work,
Waking up and going to school
So I can bully that one person
And make it all go away.
Arriving at school and seeing that one person
Now I might walk over and push him to the ground.
What a baby, he is crying
Oh no, the principal is looking at me
Now I am getting called into the principal's office
I felt so good when pushing him over
Now I feel like I got all the anger out of me,
But I don't care
But my parents are going to hit me so hard,
I will probably not show up to school tomorrow.

Lexie Price (12)
Bryngwyn Comprehensive School, Llanelli

Why Me?

Hearing them talking behind me
The whispers going through my head
About what clothes I wear
And how cheap my shoes are
Getting up after them tripping me up
I can see them looking at me
Planning something
Something to do with me.

When they arrive at school
I run
I hide
Hoping they don't see me
Lunchtime hiding in the bathroom
Eating my food
When they follow me
Down the lane
I start shaking
I run
I hide
But still they find me.

While they are punching me,
I think to myself;
Why me?

Sophia Lloyd (13)
Bryngwyn Comprehensive School, Llanelli

Through The Eyes Of A Detective

A call from the phone from the Captain
Dispatched to the crime scene of a family murder
The sound of shouting and crying as I walk through the door of the house
Four bodies lying dead on the floor, a mum, a dad and two children
The smell of blood sent shivers down my spine
The murder weapon is in an evidence bag
A taste of suspicion stuck in my throat
A feeling that something is missing
Foggy memories from last night start to appear
The panic started to appear
Where was I last night?
Did it happen again?

Libby Davies (13)
Bryngwyn Comprehensive School, Llanelli

Thou Art A Witch

"Thou art a witch!"
My husband cried as I ran out of the house.
The men soon came, and I ran in vain,
As the rain fell through the sky.
I wept and wept in the cell I was kept,
A pin pricked in my neck.
As dawn came I begged in pain for my throat ached,
From the wails of my previous jail.
The sun shone down, while I did frown,
Tied to my wooden grave, the stake alight,
I cry in fright while I ignite,
The last word I heard, as my ears burnt.
"Thou art not a witch!"

Poppy Wilson (13)
Bryngwyn Comprehensive School, Llanelli

Slavery

Breaking my back from dawn to dusk
This is my life but for freedom, I lust.
Day in, day out, I'm put to the floor,
Rotten and evil right down to their core.
Let me live my life, let me spread my wings,
Let me taste every spice and let it sting.
Let me cook food, find the love of my life,
Teach my kids how to fly a kite.
I will watch myself grow old, my kids have kids
That is my dream yet my cruel reality forbids
Give me a wish and this will all end
Let me close my eyes and lay down my head.

Dylan Montenegro-Hopkins (13)
Bryngwyn Comprehensive School, Llanelli

Untitled

They pick me up and then they get bored of me,
I watch as they choose another book;
Am I not interesting enough for you?
The young girl began to read the new book,
She looked for something more interesting,
This hurt my feelings a bit.
I haven't had someone choose me in ages,
It's sad being ignored or pushed away,
But as Dory once said, "Just keep swimming."
I will never give up my hope or courage,
I know someone will choose me someday.

Livia Marchant (12)
Bryngwyn Comprehensive School, Llanelli

I Am A Jew

I'm tired and weak,
I'm scared for my life,
The pain I go through every day,
is so unimaginable for the least to say.

My loved ones disappear,
Within the blink of an eye,
I hope I'm not next, I'm not ready to die.

I just want to go home,
Why can't all this be over?
Why am I here? What did I do?

This is like hell,
Right here on Earth,
I miss my wife,
In fact, I miss my old life.

Joshua Davies (13)
Bryngwyn Comprehensive School, Llanelli

Never-Ending Cycle

At the crack of dawn,
My cycle starts,
I must pick the cotton
Cut the cane
Feed the kids
Clean the mess
While being abused, beaten, and assaulted by
The Master.
Then, eventually, repeat it all over again.
My aching, overworked body screams for help,
But nobody cares to listen.
I'm pushed and pushed and the edge is getting
Closer but they don't stop.
But that's just life,
At least for me, it is.

Maisie Riley (13)
Bryngwyn Comprehensive School, Llanelli

We're Ruining The Planet

Polar bears are dying
Birds aren't flying
Animals are becoming extinct
Ships will start to sink
And pollute the ocean.
Earth is being burned by the sun.
This isn't fun.
Or funny.
Bees aren't producing enough honey.
Deforestation is ruining our planet,
This makes me want to vomit.
Crops won't be growing
No more water for rowing
Sea levels are rising
This isn't surprising.
We need to act soon.
Or the Earth will pop like a balloon.

Marysia Turko (13)
Bryngwyn Comprehensive School, Llanelli

I Am A Jew

Soldiers pushing, shoving us,
Children crying, clinging to their parents,
Gunshots are shot, dogs howling,
Bodies scattered on the ground,
Desperation in the air,
People begging for food, there is none;
Family members disappearing.
Where are they?
I don't know where I am,
Someone, please help me.
My legs are numb, I can't move;
What have we done to deserve this?
I am a Jew.

Kayla Hinkin (13)
Bryngwyn Comprehensive School, Llanelli

We're Killing The Earth...

We're killing the Earth and it's 'really fun',
No one can take it, not even the sun,
Sea levels are rising,
And icebergs are melting,
Even after that, no one is helping!

Our forests are turning to ashes in seconds,
How can we make any corrections?
We can't afford to lose species,
Global warming increased by two degrees,
Our future's stolen and we're the thieves...

Aleksandra Wawrzyszuk
Bryngwyn Comprehensive School, Llanelli

The Land Of Second Chances

I am returned to the land of second chances,
Although this is my 100th time coming here
I have not returned unscathed,
My lilac fur overrun with pink stitches.
Each unflattering thread adds a vine to my heart,
Constricting and covering my feelings with thorns.
Maybe my next friend will help me,
Maybe this is my last visit to this graveyard.

Poppy Whitehead (14)
Bryngwyn Comprehensive School, Llanelli

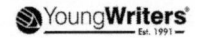

Teddy Bear

I remember the sounds.
Joy and laughter.
I remember the tea parties.
Drinking nothing from porcelain cups.
I remember her youth.
When she was happy.
I don't want to remember her cry.
I don't know why.
I remember when she put me away.
She'd grown up, she doesn't remember.
I remember her.

Cerys Stannard (14)
Bryngwyn Comprehensive School, Llanelli

The Life Of A Tank

Terror and fear are all I cause
A tank is what I am – a machine bred for war
Humans are using me to win their battles and wars
Hearing terror and distress in their screams
It causes me sadness, even though I'm a machine
After the war is over, they dump me in the wasteland
I used to call home.

Mikey Thomas (13)
Bryngwyn Comprehensive School, Llanelli

The Eyes Of A Missing Girl

I wake up,
In the middle of the forest,
Not knowing where I am,
Surrounded by trees, branches and leaves,
Walking around trying to find something,
But there's nothing other than trees,
It's like I am stuck,
In the middle of nowhere,
And no way of escaping,
I am the missing girl.

Lexi Rees (13)
Bryngwyn Comprehensive School, Llanelli

The End

As I watch on the world
There is one main thing I learned
The world is heading straight for the worse
The world is starting to need some works
Ignorant litterers
Foolish murderers
Mindless humans
The list goes on
Yet, there is still no change
The world is ending.

Lewis Thomas (13)
Bryngwyn Comprehensive School, Llanelli

The Front Line

As we approached the enemy position,
Watching infantry getting gunned down,
I gave the order for my crew to retreat,
Fearing that we'd get overrun.
As our enemy shall land over the bank,
Completely destroying the heavy bank,
I watched in terror as the enemy attacked.

Dewi Morgan (13)
Bryngwyn Comprehensive School, Llanelli

The View Of A Rugby Ball

I see a pitch full of cheer,
One by one, I watch my friends disappear,
Off they go, into the abyss,
Hoping I will not be next.
Seeing my friends in fear,
Makes me want to shed a tear.
While we wait for the game to end,
Some of us are playing dead (flat).

Llŷr Barrett (13)
Bryngwyn Comprehensive School, Llanelli

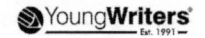

The Life Of A WWI Soldier

Training all day
Training all night
No time to rest
No time to eat
Slaughter left and right
Only a single road filled with death lies ahead
Constantly vigilant
Always without a friend
Always alone
In a world of carnage, death and chaos.

Daniel Griffiths (13)
Bryngwyn Comprehensive School, Llanelli

Life Of A Lonely Pen

As a pen, life is hard
As a pen, life is lonely
I could be the pen that makes a difference
But a pen's life is short
During my life, I am chewed
And chucked around
Just to be put in a dark case
And to be binned
And lost
And forgotten
I am a pen.

Alfie Hartnell (13)
Bryngwyn Comprehensive School, Llanelli

Henry

Where is my ball? I sigh,
Mummy's thrown it too far,
It is too hard to find,
I look, I look, and I look for as long as I can,
Until Mummy calls me in,
That ball will forever remain in my brain.

Skye Rance-Williams (12)
Bryngwyn Comprehensive School, Llanelli

The Sad Clown

The flashing lights shine brightly in my eyes,
Performing the next big act, I realise,
The children cry at my sad, pale face,
My heart is wrenched, and I finish with pace.

I've learned quickly what I shouldn't do,
I shouldn't feel empathy, shouldn't I have known,
My heart would wrench, I'd feel like screaming,
Tears form, but no one knows what I'm feeling.

The act is done, all of it finished,
The mirror stares at me, my make-up diminished,
My pale face torments me, my anger inside,
I smash the mirror, no one can hide.

I run outside the tears still there,
I turn, a child stares at me, though nothing would bear,
She's smiling at me, her cheeks pink and warm,
My wrenched heart eases, the end of the storm.

Eva Taylor (12)
Notley High School & Braintree Sixth Form, Braintree

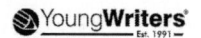

Too Many To Please

Every day is a different story
what's right is wrong
and what's wrong is right
I must make the right decision
I must have all the glory

I'm being pulled one way
but also dragged another
I have to please everyone
Is it even possible?
I'm just hoping for the perfect day

They want me to be
something I'm not
why can't everyone understand?
It's like I'm trapped
with nothing but a dream to be free

Wherever I go
I'm a different person
like clothes from a wardrobe
Each day I must choose
Which personality I'm going to show

My parents, I try to make proud
My peers, I try to make laugh
My teachers, I try to impress
I can't be myself
I want to let my voice scream loud

I'm done being your Barbie
You can't dress me anymore
I've had enough with the masks
Look at me for who I am
Must my name be written on my head in Sharpie?

I can't do this any longer
I can't be the best of both worlds
I'm tired of pretending
I'm not acting like I'm okay

I'm done being tough
I'm done, I'm done, I'm done.

Amelie Leader (14)
Notley High School & Braintree Sixth Form, Braintree

A Teenager's Truth

'Everyone has a purpose' how is that true?
Lying is all I see in this life
so why would this not follow through?

Sat in the corner of my broken home,
at peace knowing one day I will finally be alone,
here and there, Monday to Friday, I'm everywhere.

Working hard to never disappoint those who surround me,
whilst I'm still stuck on the time when I was once happy.
It seems too far away,
not knowing if I will ever get there.

The voices in my head screaming at me
I don't know what to do anymore, I'm struggling
to breathe,
Sometimes, I consider if it would be easier if
there were two of me,
I wonder whether the hardships of this world were
made for me,

I'm not able to scream or shout
stuck on the floor crying out,
I've never heard or seen
just a normal teenage girl who seems at peace.

The smiles, the laughs are all fake,
as I step into the gates of school
I have to forget about my past trauma and put up a wall.

The stress of school fills my head
as I lie down in the only place my mind gets to rest,
before I have to repeat this all again.

Faith Gibson (13)
Notley High School & Braintree Sixth Form, Braintree

The One They Adore

I wake up, another beautiful,
The primates still lounging around,
I wake them, they need to work,
Those savage simians need to learn from me,
Prestigious, perfect and powerful,
I'm the one they adore!

The scruffy, frightened man slouches in,
Weak and pitiful, poor thing,
He dumps the slop and grain for the others,
Then tries to swiftly leave,
I aim the projectile at him,
Perfect hit as always,
He waves at me with a crude gesture,
I just smile as I feast on my delicacy,
He's the one I adore,
As he's so fun,

Finally, the paparazzi rolls in,
Passing by on their sluggish cart,
There I lay, on the sun-baked stone.
Searched calmly with innocence in my eyes,
As the flock saw my perfect body,
I relished in it all,
Time after time,
More and more of the public came,
More and more love for my pristine self,

But as the day raged onward,
And the sky's sphere shifts out of sight,
Less and less humans came,
But that doesn't bother me,
As the next day will come,
I'm the one they adore.

Thomas Ross (13)
Notley High School & Braintree Sixth Form, Braintree

Bukayo Saka

The ball was set on the ground,
He had to score,
Saka was shining with confidence,
The only person that could stop him was the Italian keeper,
He took a deep breath,
Took three steps back,
He had an entire country on his shoulders,
He had over sixty million English people,
Relying on him,
He had a world watching him,
There he stood,
The bravest teenager of all time,
The bravest boy in England.

There he stood,
One kick away from winning the Euros,
He ran up,
The world held its breath,
Bang!
Saka had shot.

Saka had missed,
The best teenager had missed,
The world went silent,
The best teenager had missed the penalty to win.

His teammates went rushing over,
Racial abuse was thrown at him wherever he went,
Online,
Even in public,
Saka's confidence was at an all-time low,
After all, he was just a kid.

Two years later,
Saka was back,
All his confidence was back,
Single-handedly getting Arsenal Champions
League football,
He is simply the best.

Jacob Clayton (12)
Notley High School & Braintree Sixth Form, Braintree

I Am The Earth

I am the Earth,
Sick and dying,
People poison me.

All around I see humans dying,
They are refugees,
Hope has fled them, just like their families,
Nowhere to be seen.
Few try to help them,
In that sense, they're like me,
I can never stop myself feeling
Sorry for the refugees.

Every dusk and every dawn,
People cut my trees,
Their hearts of stone so bitter;
They don't have any mercy,
For every tree they cut,
They kill an innocent monkey.

Every night, people hurt and harm,
Just to get money,
If you could look through my eyes,
You wouldn't believe what you see.

Something has to be different,
So everyone is free,
You must be the change you wish to see in the world;
These are the wise words of Mahatma Gandhi.

I am the Earth,
Sick and dying,
Can somebody save me?

Deniz Saribal (12)
Notley High School & Braintree Sixth Form, Braintree

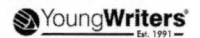

My Guinea Pigs' Feelings

C ome here
O pen my cage
O pen the bag
K eep my ball filled with hay
I love you
E ven though you

C an put food in my cage
R uin my day
U are amazing
M y best owner
B ut we love you
L ike you
E at and give us food

And even though

B lackberry gets more attention
L ike what about us
A re we just for show?
C ookie and I get less time with you
K eep on getting him out
B ut leaving us in the cage
E ating food
R unning around bored
R udely ignoring us
Y eah we have feelings too

W ater
A nd
L ove
N othing but
U being kind, and loving us
T hanks, love you Mum x

Jessica Stammers (11)
Notley High School & Braintree Sixth Form, Braintree

Dancing In The Shadows

In the shadows, she danced with grace
a backup dancer in her rightful place
but little did they know, she had a spark
a talent that could light up the dark

With every step, she stole the show
her moves so captivating, they had to know
the spotlight followed her every move
as she grooved and twirled in her own groove

Her presence on stage, a force to be reckoned
as she stole the spotlight, leaving others second
no longer just a backup, she shone so bright
a star in her own right, stealing the night

So let's cheer for the backup dancer's might
for stealing the spotlight with all her might
she proved that dreams can become reality
and even in the shadows, we can find our clarity.

Amy Rayfield (13)
Notley High School & Braintree Sixth Form, Braintree

Orca

Bound in a measly tank,
I am no more than their money bank,
Eighty-six feet, small and tied,
Missing the ocean, large and wide.

They say I'm just a simple beast,
A spectacle, a show to feast,
My dorsal fin once strong and proud,
Now droops with sorrow, no longer allowed.

In the reflection once roared a majestic, powerful whale,
But I'm a mere attraction, trapped in this jail,
Robbed of my family, my pod, my kin,
Gone is my freedom and spirit within.

Human greed, my captor's desire,
Leaving me feeling nothing but ire,
Here I am, scarred from this tragedy,
Help me evade their brutality.

Grace Clark (11)
Notley High School & Braintree Sixth Form, Braintree

Barricaded

Locked, dark and isolated.
Wooden boards obstruct the door with caution,
Waiting to dissolve any attempt of freedom.
The rigid, abrasive floor scraped,
Jabbed and picked at her knees and elbows,
Ripping through her skin.
She had become a prisoner.
Yet she was not a criminal.
In her childhood basement, she lay,
The imaginary monsters she made up in her youth
Now coming to life.
So desolate, yet so close to bliss.
Echoes of children's laughter
Crept into the vents of the cell.
Her mastermind's plan was woven with steel thread.
Unescapable and intricately sewn.
There was slim chance of escape.

Ava Cataldo (13)
Notley High School & Braintree Sixth Form, Braintree

Through Their Eyes - Refugees

R eluctantly my life was taken from me
E verything was perfect
F rom my home to an unknown
U nknowingly I didn't know my life was going to be tough
G one away to start a new chapter
E ven though the life I left was prodigious
E verything is going to change.

R esistantly the border passed me by
E stablished my role in the world
F inding myself alone and afraid
U nder this unknown land and language
G oing nowhere and everywhere at the same time
E ven the world had been misled
E verything was gone.

Alice Loveard (14)
Notley High School & Braintree Sixth Form, Braintree

Brighter Day For Me

I feel lonely,
Like no one is around,
Darkness overtakes me.
Pulling me to the ground,
I cry out great tears,
I'm drowning in the sea!
But then I just remember,
There is a brighter day for me.

I open my eyes to sunlight,
I do have friends! All around,
There is joy everywhere,
The happiest ever sound,
I smile, I am not lonely!
Now I can finally see,
No matter what happens,
There is a brighter day for me.

So take a great breath, do you finally see?
There is always a brighter day,
A brighter day for you and me!

Millie-Rose Cunnane (12)
Notley High School & Braintree Sixth Form, Braintree

Jungle

The jungle was decaying
All the animals were raging
The greenery withered
While the river shivered
The treetops groan with the beating sun
While the other existing trees have been hung
Hung from the other trees that have been taken
Maybe that's why people are so shaken
Shaken from the fact the malnourished jungle
Has been demolished for others to be humble
Animals' homes have been turned into decoration
Lots of them have suffered a separation
People protest about the demolition
Companies stare and grimace at the protestation.

Alex Frost (12)
Notley High School & Braintree Sixth Form, Braintree

Mirror

She stares, she looks, she weeps.
Crying, all because of me.
Her face smudged and smeared as can be.
Her reflection staring back at me.
No one here
No one knows
She rips and peels and picks away
At the features I have shown her.
And one day, one night
I will watch her go.
In her room.
On her own.
For me to sit and watch.
I had done it
I reflected on what she hated.
I gave her a picture.
I painted it
I'm sorry
But I can't help it,
I will never be good enough
She stared, she looked, she wept.

Darcy Miller (14)
Notley High School & Braintree Sixth Form, Braintree

Anne Frank

In an attic, above the stairs
been hiding there for days
got a notepad
looking everywhere
hoping to find somewhere to go
knocking on the door
massive footstep
coming upstairs,
hear talking, comes the light
see three men standing high
in cuffs walking somewhere
In a prison or somewhere
in different clothes, haven't washed my hair
I've been stranded here for days
The door opens, a man stands there
telling us to go over there
I can't move, I feel sick
my eyes close and I die in here.

Harry Etheridge (13)
Notley High School & Braintree Sixth Form, Braintree

On The Farm

We're all slower,
As time tick-tocks our companions lie,
Starstruck in their groves,
On the farm I see,
This is not what we are supposed to be.

The crops eventually grown,
The animals faintly roam,
Another day on the farm,
Is another day at harm,
I can see,
This is not what we are supposed to be.

The time has a core,
The end of my life has begun,
Who would think that the last thing I'll see,
Is a butcher's knife,
Running inside of me.

Elliott Barry (12)
Notley High School & Braintree Sixth Form, Braintree

Marmite

Sitting all alone, with no friends in sight,
Full of fright, waiting endlessly,
The cupboard opens, but I'm always the last picked,
I'm left till last, why?
Is it the way I look? Is it my foul taste?
Is it my freaky smell? What could it be?
Why does no one like me?
I'm a jar of Marmite!
The embarrassment I feel with my yellow lid for a hat,
A glass jar coloured black,
If I was a clear pot,
Maybe I would have more friends,
Again - I'm a jar of Marmite.

Eva Tammaro (13)
Notley High School & Braintree Sixth Form, Braintree

Story Of Anne Frank

One day when the sun shone bright
They took away our fun and light
Because of my religion, because I am a Jew
I don't think that's very fair, do you?
Maybe if I was not born this way
The world would stand still and not sway
I sit here and write a diary
My anger, red and fiery
If only things could be equal
If this story had a different sequel
Dear reader, I must accept my fate
Trapped inside this imaginary crate of despair
Ask yourself, is this fair?

Erin Guilder (11)
Notley High School & Braintree Sixth Form, Braintree

Hidden Behind A Screen

I never wanted to make people insecure
I started because I liked it
As times changed, I changed
Now I do everything for likes
And views and comments
I'm trapped in a cage
With no way out
I try to give people joy
Instead I give them grief

Sometimes I wonder
What kind of world we live in
Where people can hate through a screen
But never say things to your face
So I hide behind my screen
Hoping someday things will be better.

Fleur Thatcher (11)
Notley High School & Braintree Sixth Form, Braintree

Climate Change

No one listens
as the melting ice caps glisten.
Climate change needs to stop
as bits of ice begin to drop.

Once a winter story,
Somewhere, sometimes in its glory,
Burning away the green of the seasons,
for nothing but just reasons.

Now they sleep beneath the heaters burning
None have survived the long days of learning
Dreams to wake are long forgotten
Nothing is left but cotton.

Emily Kemp (14)
Notley High School & Braintree Sixth Form, Braintree

Marmite

As I get out some bread
I no longer need to dread
because I know I'm about to be fed

Hastily get out the toaster
I take every opportunity to boast her
the bread is as soft as fur

As my newfound toast starts to burn
I can't help but to learn
that it is the Marmite that I yearn

In the cupboard, I go
for the Marmite starts to show
and on the toast, it goes.

Luke Garraghan (14)
Notley High School & Braintree Sixth Form, Braintree

Ukrainian Refugee

We were rushed out of the house
Lucky we were
Bombs darkened the sky
It was all a blur
Once a place for the family
Now left in ruin
Many memories lost
To this pointless war
We were rushed to the car
Smoke filled our lungs
Bombs rained down
Destroying our city of hope
All our lives lost
To this pointless war
We were bound to die
In this pointless war.

Daniel Smith (11)
Notley High School & Braintree Sixth Form, Braintree

Love

When I was young, I never understood
How love could hurt
I loved the things that made me frown

As I grew up, I realised
Nothing is as painful as love!

Even when it stings, I chase it
I squeeze it in my hands
Until my fingers bleed
Even when I let it go
I forget about the pain
And only remember the warmth

Love
A tragically, beautiful thing.

Jamie Smith (13)
Notley High School & Braintree Sixth Form, Braintree

The Animal Kingdom

Our oceans were crystal clear,
Now us sea creatures shed tears.
Half of our creatures have died,
Not even one fisherman has dared to cry.
Now all of our breeds have bred,
Half of our oceans are stained red.
No one has cared, not even a soul,
And we can't tell our story to be told.
Lots of people aren't scared of us,
But lots of people just cuss about us.

Bella Browning (12)
Notley High School & Braintree Sixth Form, Braintree

Climate Change

I searched and searched for food
My hunger grew and grew
The food somehow vanished
But I never knew

I tugged and squirmed trying to get free
I was in pain, what a misery
Would I get out of this horrible thing
Or would I stay like this forever
Regretting everything?

Please put your litter in the bin
It will only take a moment of your time.

Imogen Sibley (12)
Notley High School & Braintree Sixth Form, Braintree

Rosa Parks

I am Rosa Parks.
As I step on the bus,
frail and shivering,
I am Rosa Parks.
As I find my seat,
their beady eyes upon me.
I am Rosa Parks.
As they ask me to move,
and I refuse.
I am Rosa Parks.
Even as I am arrested,
as small as an ant.
I am Rosa Parks.
The mother
of the freedom movement.

Michelle Sarpong (11)
Notley High School & Braintree Sixth Form, Braintree

Struck Dead

I helped you to survive.
I drove off the enemies.
I am the reason you are you.
I witnessed my friends die.
For you to be alive.
My courage and bravery.
Helped you to be alive.
But I was unlucky,
The floor came rushing to me.
As the bullet struck my side.
And death gave me a friendly wave.

Benedict Todd (11)
Notley High School & Braintree Sixth Form, Braintree

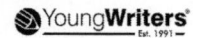

We Must Act Now

Through their eyes,
There is the sky,
Big and blue,
Like the sea too.

There they stand,
Looking at the land,
Falling apart,
Bit by bit,
Through their teeth grit.

Icebergs are melting,
Drip, drip...
How do the animals survive?
Soon they will lose their lives!

Zack Haywood (12)
Notley High School & Braintree Sixth Form, Braintree

Until We Meet Again

T earing up as soon as I lost you
R ealising you're in a better place
I wish I could still see your face
S ometimes I know you're there with me
T ill we meet again
A tough time without you
N ight, god bless, and sweet dreams my brother.

Harvey Green (11)
Notley High School & Braintree Sixth Form, Braintree

Climate Change, Global Warming

The ice crashed into the waters
The heat slaughters
The dangers of life are in your hands
So don't make any wrong plans
Climate change was here first
So don't make it worse
Life here is precious
So don't make it dangerous.

Lia Dicker (12)
Notley High School & Braintree Sixth Form, Braintree

Through The Eyes Of A Prisoner

I saw the disappointment on my mum's face,
And the anger in my dad's eyes,
The flashing lights blinded me,
As the strains played in my head,
I felt the cold metal of the handcuffs being
Placed around my wrist,
Am I now a prisoner?

Darcie Cross (12)
Notley High School & Braintree Sixth Form, Braintree

Marmite's Life

I stand there all alone
a full open jar
I get pushed away,
from my enemy Nutella,
always getting picked
leaving me in there
I feel so alone
I don't know what to do
I might rot away
if I'm not used
oh, help me.

Sophie Curzon (12)
Notley High School & Braintree Sixth Form, Braintree

World War II
A kennings poem

Trench digger
Gun wielder
Base defender
Enemy slayer
Uniform wearer
Rations eater
Plane flyer
Lice picker
Helmet wearer
Bomb dropper
Team player

I'm a WWII pilot.

Jake Haley (11)
Notley High School & Braintree Sixth Form, Braintree

Ronaldinho

R espect
O n top
N ever give up
A spiration
L oyal
D esire
I nspiring
N ever back down
H ero
O riginal.

Logan Freemantle (11)
Notley High School & Braintree Sixth Form, Braintree

WWII Fighter
A kennings poem

Lice picker
Mice eater
Cat chaser
Ground digger
Gun runner
Tank driver
Soldier fighter.

Katie Kemp (12)
Notley High School & Braintree Sixth Form, Braintree

The Seasons

Seasons come and seasons go
The winter invariably brings snow
The snow falls from the dark and dreary sky
But menacing clouds often drift away
Leaving us a clear and frosty day.

But in winter we can get nice and cosy
Children playing with cheeks so rosy
Tobogganing and characterful snowmen building
That melts with the rays of the watery sun
Children sleep that night with dreams of fun.

Seasons come and seasons go
The springtime river waters flow
They start to glisten with the long-awaited sun
But the cold of winter has not long gone
As the young sparrows start to sing their song.

The cheerful yellow daffodils start to bloom
The arrival of the baby lambs will follow soon
The Easter bunny brings chocolate eggs in abundance
To the excited young and expectant old
Hunting for the special eggs wrapped in gold.

Seasons come and seasons go
The summer sun puts on a show
Bees and butterflies show off their beauty
The grass dries out like parched straw
The fast-flowing streams are no more.

Lollies and ice creams become a daily treat
The scorching sand burns the children's feet
The cool, calm and inviting seas that were once deserted
Are now filled with children surfing the waves
While adults are enjoying warm, long, lazy days.

Seasons come and seasons go
The autumn leaves blow to and fro
The children crush the dried-out leaves
As they return to school looking tidy and smart
Ready for the new term to start.

Luminous fireworks light up the sky
"Oooohhh!" and "Aaaahhh!" the spectators cry
It's the 5th of November and the year is drawing to a close
The seasons come and the seasons go
Sometimes fast and sometimes slow.

Isabella Dean (11)
The King John School, Thundersley

Through Taylor Swift's Eyes

In my eyes, a world unfolds,
Where stories bloom and hearts are told.
Each day begins with a blank space,
A canvas waiting for my grace.

Through my eyes, the city gleams,
In 'Welcome to New York', it seems.
I see the lights, the hustle, the crowd,
Where dreams are whispered, and hope's allowed.

In 'Shake It Off', I find my stride,
In every setback, I won't hide.
Through my eyes, resilience gleams,
In every setback, in every scheme.

'Blank Space' reveals a different view,
In every heartache, love shines through.
I see the masks, the hidden fears,
In every laughter, in every tears.

Through my eyes, the seasons turn,
In 'August', memories burn.
I see the sweetness tinged with sorrow,
In every today, in every tomorrow.

In 'Love Story', I find my muse,
In every heartbeat, I won't lose.
I see the magic of love's embrace,
In every moment, in every chase.

'Red' paints the passion I hold dear,
In every longing, I draw near.
I see the colours, vibrant and bright,
In every day, in every night.

Through my eyes, the world's a stage,
In 'The Man', I turn the page.
I see the struggles, the fight for rights,
In every wrong, in every height.

In my gaze, the stories intertwine,
In every lyric, a tale is divine.
Through my eyes, we see the art,
In every beat, I claim her part.

Hollie Tidiman (14)
The King John School, Thundersley

The Beauty Of Humanity

In my galaxy, my world, my home,
Are my dear planets: there to keep me from not being alone,
Among the sweltering Venus, frosty Neptune and Jupiter with its monumental girth,
I dare say that I have a favourite planet and that is my dear Earth,

For the most unique of planets is she,
With her bursting land to her flowing sea,
But what I adore her for is her most different of features,
The humans - her most intelligent creatures,

Each with their own beautiful set of profile and mind,
A personality that can be clever, strong or kind,
I often find them admiring me as well, from my rise to my set,
It always delights me that they do not think of me as a threat,

I excite myself by thinking maybe I can be one of them,
So, to fit in, I shine their home up like one of their own precious gems,
I kiss the plump cheeks of joyous children playing within my warmth,
I raise the bountiful supply of plants and flora, they kindly for me bring forth,

I watch the quiet love-filled moments everyone will forget,
but I never will.
A cheering joke or a passionate kiss in the autumn's first
chill,
Sticky, tiny fingers cling to a mother's flowy sleeve,
Hushed whispers of promises, to never leave,

Yes, Earth has the highest of mountains and the deepest of
oceans, but neither truly compare above,
The beauty of humanity with its joy and with its love.

Isabel Cole (13)
The King John School, Thundersley

Step Up

As I melt, the azure waters glisten around me,
Rising high, yet sad and worrying;
When will it stop?

I see the pain it's giving to the world,
Though, no fault of its own,
Climate change evokes pain in the world;
When will it stop?

Soon, I will be gone.
Soon, my icicle friends will be gone.
Soon, we will be gone.
Soon...

Will humankind step up and save me?
And save the world?
Without your change,
I will be gone as rapidly as lightning strikes,
Soon, coastal towns will disappear,
As rapidly as lightning strikes.

Humankind has to step up,
Step up to save me,
Humankind has to step up,
Step up and save the world.

Harry Wilson (12)
The King John School, Thundersley

Just Like Me

Scared every day, countless nights with no sleep
A lovely night's dream, I'm sure I'll be guaranteed
Bombs bursting through walls, I hug my brother tight
On the TV, I see a dreadful war going on tonight

I hear screams and cries outside, knowing it's not safe
I listen to the news, comfortable by the fireplace
When will it end? Why can peace not be made?
I feel bad for these kids, they're probably afraid

My stomach rumbles, an empty numbness pains through me
Mother asks if we want dinner which we all agree
My home is broken in pieces, full of rubble and suffer
I watch little children in dust and dirt, which makes me shudder

I've lost everything, my parents, my loved ones, my childhood
I ask Father if I can go play later in the neighbourhood

I pray the war ends,
I pray my brother and I survive,
I pray for help and notice,
I pray my country is fine,

I want to cry no more tears, may God guide us
I wonder if all children are just like us?

Suraya Siddique (13)
The King John School, Thundersley

Fairy-Tale Murder

Clutching the fairy godmother's wand, I proceed to step towards the sink
Glancing back over to who once was my Prince Charming, staring right at me, and doesn't blink
Strawberry jam trickles down my fingertips
"No woman has the power to kill her husband"
I laugh and grin, as the knife clatters down, down on the worktop

The ambivalent butterflies die inside me
This is the story, this is what it's meant to be
I am the princess, and he's the sleeping apparition

Touching up my appearance, I stare back at myself at my reflection
I am a cheerful young lady who has a gorgeous face and heart, that's what everyone sees
Silence creeps over my apartment as the light above flickers like it is being infested by weeds
No more roses or freshly baked pies
Is this a fairy tale in everyone's eyes?
I look around and then down
Blood splattered across my freshly washed gown
My eyes widen in horror
What do I do? What if I'm found?

Washing away the guilt in the steaming shower, it is like I've been drowned in boiling water, I'm scarred for life
This feeling...
Is never leaving
Questions and thoughts engulfed as realisation hits
This is no fairy tale?
This is not what it's meant to be
I am the beast, he's the sleeping beauty.

Madison Alsop (13)
The King John School, Thundersley

Dog's Poem

In the heart of the home where the warm winds blow,
Lives a dog named Oscar, with a heart aglow.
With paws like whispers on the morning ground,
He trots through life with joy unbound.

"My humans are great, they're the stars in my sky,
They feed me, they lead me and never ask why.
With every wag, I try to show,
The love I have, the gratitude I owe.

The park is my kingdom, the grass my throne,
Among the trees and breezes, I'm never alone.
Chasing balls, leaping high,
Underneath the vast, open sky.

At night, I dream of endless fields,
Of bones and treats, and all the yields.
But most of all, it's my family I see,
In every dream, they're there with me.

So here's a bark, a woof, a tail-wagging song,
With my humans by my side, nothing can go wrong.
In their company, my spirit soars,
For they're the world I so adore."

This is the tale of Oscar, happy and bright,
With a heart full of love, shining light.
In his eyes, the simplest truth we can glean,
In the love of a dog, life's beauty is seen.

James McGettigan (14)
The King John School, Thundersley

Numb

Through their eyes, it's over,
Been and gone,
Left on the battlefield.

Through their eyes,
It's just a place,
A landmark in history,
A wavelength in the spectrum of light that
Our lives are judged by.

But then, they're not me.

It was difficult at first,
Trying to live with what I'd done,
Trying to mull over and mould the emotion
I feel into a positive.

Because what is positive?
What can render me happy?
What can make me feel again?

At first, I felt human,
More human than human,
A person,
A useful part of a working unit,
Yet conflict led to war... then to bloodshed,

So here I am,
A thousand miles from home,
And a million miles from who I was.

What right have I to feel?
What right have I to be?
What right have I to live?
When I had snatched that very gift from many,
As cold as the blood strung through my fingers,
As numb and emotionally unaware as the toddler
I could have fathered,
So what was this all for?

Francesca Vigilante (16)
The King John School, Thundersley

Alone

Footsteps, one by one getting further,
Conversations slowly turned into a murmur.
I hear the familiar click of the door,
Then the engine revs, they're gone I'm sure.
I begin to cry, I begin to whimper,
In my isolated surroundings with just a blanket and a slipper.

My cry turns into a bark, my whimper turns into a howl,
Louder and louder they must be able to hear me now.
I lie on my blanket while time goes by,
They won't come back, this I deny.
I'm overwhelmed with feelings of betray,
Is this just a game they are trying to play?
Why is this happening have I done something wrong?
Surely my punishment didn't have to be this long?

I wait and I wait until I hear a sound,
A familiar click from somewhere around.
Footsteps one by one getting nearer,
Conversations becoming clearer.
My owner finally stands in front of me,
And my tail starts wagging joyfully.
As she picks me up she kisses my head,
This washes away all my sadness and dread.

Sophie Webb (14)
The King John School, Thundersley

Why? What Happened?

Friends to enemies,
You used to climb our branches, study us, care for us.
What changed?
You now destroy us, kill us, use us.
So I ask: Why? What happened?

Birds, monkeys, marsupials, apes - these live in us.
We give them shelter, warmth, and life.
Sadly, as you murder us, you murder them.
You now destroy us, kill us, use us.
So I ask: Why? What happened?

We are the lungs of your Earth, your shelter, your shade,
Your thermostat, your protector,
Your playground, your fuel.
You now destroy us, kill us, use us.
So I ask: Why? What happened?

My family once stood proudly across this land,
But now I stand alone, afraid, the monsters bearing down,
Their yellow limbs and dazzling eyes,
Crunching, cutting, crushing, I fail to comprehend it,
Even through their eyes.

You have destroyed us, killed us, used us.
So I ask again, with my final breath: Why? What happened?

Kate Williamson (14)
The King John School, Thundersley

The Other Kid

I think everything is perfect,
But this kid, he shows me no respect,
He never leaves me be,
I don't think he can see,
The hurt he causes me,
Acting as if the school is his,
You'd think he's got a perfect life,
But it's filled with pain and strife.

Imagine being late,
Because you woke up at eight,
As you're too poor to buy an alarm,
And your parents cause you harm,
Family always neglecting,
Nobody is respecting,
You.

You think your life is at its end,
But all you need is a friend,
However, you can only spread hatred,
The only thing your family demonstrated.

Everything seems hopeless,
Until the kid you never leave alone,
Shows you kindness,
While everyone stares at their phone.

Bullies are misunderstood,
With lonely eyes who want to do good,
A little kindness goes a long way,
So treat everyone with respect today.

Dylan Rott (14)
The King John School, Thundersley

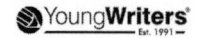

Pomegranate The Fruit Of Love

Pomegranate the fruit of love I get called,
I must be opened up with care and compassion
For the sweet seeds enclosed by my shell.
If hunger lurks and you show no love or attention,
And you tear and rip to wrench my fruit out,
If with no gentle understanding you then bare teeth and shred,
You'll be left with nothing but my mangled remnants.
Was the greediness and haste worth the red stains under your fingernails?
All for a mauled fruit?
Were you too blinded by your craving
To see the destruction you were caving?
Your ravenous yearning is the reason for the desecration of my lore.

If only you acted with affection
Then you'd get to the warmth of my heart you're so desperate for.
With patience and virtue acquiring my seeds will be achieved.
Once shown tenderness and endearment
I will share my taste for you to relish.

For I am pomegranate, the fruit of love.

Melissa Tsappis (14)
The King John School, Thundersley

A Life Of A Dog

In fields of green, where sunlight gleams,
A loyal heart, in fur it beams.
The canine soul, a joyful dance,
A furry friend, life's sweet romance.

With floppy ears and a wagging tail,
Through boundless joy, emotions sail.
In dawn's embrace or dusk's soft hue,
A faithful companion, forever true.

The leash, a link, in friendship's chain,
Bound by love, no need to feign.
Through playful bounds and fetching games,
Life's symphony, the barking claims.

Under moonlit skies, a guardian's gaze,
Through starlit nights, in loyal phase.
In every paw print, a tale unfolds,
A saga of warmth, that never folds.

Amidst the howls and midnight's song,
A four-legged friend, where love belongs.
Through rain or shine, in joy or strife,
A dog's life is poetry, in every stride.

Kye Woodruff (12)
The King John School, Thundersley

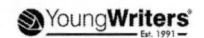

Modelling Is NOT Glamorous

I deserve new skin
Skin you haven't yet concealed, contoured, or corrected
I deserve a new upbringing
One that's safe, one that's healthy and protective
I deserve new eyes
Eyes you haven't been able to photograph, and disregard that there is anyone behind them.

You strangle and suffocate me, with fabric and material until I can't breathe
All for recognition and validation that I may not even receive
You give me a script about my life for me to read
That I do not believe but at least the audience is pleased.

I deserve a new ribcage, I deserve new shoulders
But most importantly, I do not deserve
A weight on my chest that feels like a thousand boulders
Your words, they cut deep, you left my hands stained
You painted me with my own blood, but I was scared
So I kept quiet and never complained.

Darcy Rust (14)
The King John School, Thundersley

You Brighten My Day

In the celestial ballet where night meets day,
A moon enamoured, in love's soft array.
Her silvery beams, a tender embrace,
Yet the sun's warmth remains an elusive chase.

Uncertainty weaves through their cosmic dance,
A love unspoken, an unrequited trance.
Harrowing shadows, the moon's lament,
In the sun's brilliance, her heart is spent.

She bathes in the radiance of his golden light,
Yet in his gaze, she's a distant night.
A symphony of longing in the cosmic sea,
As the sun drifts off, oblivious in his celestial spree.

In the quiet interlude between dusk and dawn,
Her love lingers, an ethereal pawn.
The sun's brilliance fades, she's all that remains,
Forever bound in unrequited laws, enduring chains.

Alina Saleemi (14)
The King John School, Thundersley

More Than Meets The Eye

(A Fan Perspective On Lin-Manuel Miranda)

There's this guy,
Lin-Manuel Miranda,
There's more than meets the eye.
Even though he's the genius behind Hamilton,
He is much more of an outstander.

Love repeated eight times,
In his Tony's sonnet,
Everyone should adore how he rhymes.

When Puerto Rico suffered,
He used his fame
And with his help, they afforded
The rebuild of their island.

'In the Heights' was his first gig,
Raising representation of the Latin,
No one knew that this
And his next project would be big.

He spreads pride,
Wearing his rainbow pin.
There is for sure more than meets the eye.
There is so much more to Lin,
With his words of inspiration.

Yes, people may be surprised
When they find out about Lin,
That there's more than meets the eye.

Rose Snook (13)
The King John School, Thundersley

A Tree's Point Of View

I'm from the garden, where everything blooms,
I stand tall within nature's room,
I reach towards the sky,
As the seasons go by.

I see it all,
Flowers big and small,
I hear trees whispering secrets
As their leaves sway.

I hear children great and small
Chase butterflies without a care at all,
Artists sit in my shade,
Their paintings adored, masterpieces made.

This is a garden of peace
Where worries and troubles find relief,
A place for reflection, where everyone can take a retreat,
Meanwhile, being within nature's heartbeat.

In this garden, I'll stand to witness
All of the world's wonders hand in hand.

Aidan Armitage (12)
The King John School, Thundersley

Bear

I'm always there for her day and night,
I'm always holding my owner tight.
I'm always sad when she goes away,
It makes her so upset why can't she stay here and play?
She tells me all the nasty things they've said,
As she lies crying on her bed.
Why do they have to be so cruel?
She used to love going to school.
Names, comments and snide looks,
At lunch, she tries to escape into her books.
She told the teachers but it made things worse,
It's like she's living with a curse.
I feel so helpless that there's nothing I can do,
So I'll hold her whilst she dreams and hope they come true.

Jessica Williamson (11)
The King John School, Thundersley

8:23

Dear those who I love the most,
I fear the inevitable is creeping close,
Day by day, night by night,
I feel myself slipping away, losing this fight.

The light at the end of my tunnel began to dim,
As my chances of survival only grew slim,
I hated you seeing me in such a state,
So I locked my emotions away and forgot to communicate.

Let my funeral be filled with colour and glee,
And celebrate the fact my soul is free,
I would hate to leave this world without being honest,
So my dying wish is for you to remember tomorrow isn't promised.

Yours sincerely the girl in the trees,
As the time of death was 8:23

Ava Dowler (14)
The King John School, Thundersley

Aftershave

A s I scanned the shelves, I came across your presence.
F or me, it was the unique design of the bottle which caught my eye.
T aking a closer look, the shape of the bottle reminded me of some good times.
E ver so quickly, I sprayed my wrist and the scent of lavender filled the air.
R ealising the fragrance was one that could make my memories come alive.
S uddenly, the cool, cold sensation across my wrist felt like the coolness of ice.
H ow is this possible?
A fter all, this is only liquid in a bottle.
V acant on your wrist, it's like a flower without its scent.
E verlasting!

Harry Thompson (12)
The King John School, Thundersley

Change

Change means different
Change is hard
Hard to say goodbye
Hard to move on

But don't worry, change is good
Good to try new things
Good to learn who you are

We will all go through change good or bad
Sometimes for the better
Some for the wost
We don't always get to choose
Sometimes we do

I am change
I am different
Good
And bad

You are change
You are different
Good
And bad

We are change
We are different
Good
And bad

We all go through change
No matter who we are
Good
And bad.

Evie Rott (11)
The King John School, Thundersley

Freedom - MohBad Remembered

I want to be free, oh freedom
I want to escape wisely, oh wisdom
Every day, I look at the soldiers, they are very thick.
I wish I could fight them but I'm weak
If I get caught, I'll be killed.
If I don't get caught, I'll be filled with joy

I want to be free, oh freedom,
Look at those birds on the tree
I wish I could be like them, if I was free
Now there is an attack!
They are all shooting
My mind is rebooting.
Wondering that I could die.
Out there I lie.
I've been shot at.
When I'm there no more.
People would love me more.

Oluwamayowa Oguntoye (12)
The King John School, Thundersley

A Day Through The Eyes Of A Tiger

I wake up to a warm summer breeze,
I soak up the rays into my orange and black skin,
I stand up and stretch my furry legs,
What a lovely day for hunting,
I run quickly to the ferns my favourite spot to hunt,
I see a rabbit family hopping in front of the dunes,
I pounce!
They scatter and I chase the plumpest one
I leap and trap it underneath my arms,
I walk back to my cave,
It is getting dark now,
I split the food between my children,
I lie down my head on my paws,
And slowly my eyelids droop until I am fast asleep.
That is what this tiger does 365 days a year.

Alfie Malby (11)
The King John School, Thundersley

A Dance Of Fire And Ice

In a universe where the fiery embers shine bright,
And the cold caverns which are as dark as night.
Both clash, sworn to be enemies,
No one would think they were destined to be.

One burns with passion, fueled with blood-soaked rage,
But provides a warm barrier, one that guides like a safe.
Silent as a still ocean and brutal enough to upset even me,
But deep inside its cold, bitter heart lies unforgettable memories.

This quarrel of lovers, the battle of friends,
It seemed like the relationship would surely end.
Never,
Their eternal dance would last forever.

Max Day (14)
The King John School, Thundersley

Valhalla Calls

V igour course through bone and skin,
A lone for no longer united with kin.
L ost winds blow the battlefield's cries,
H alls of Vikings with horns to rise.
A esir gods may they bless our axe,
L ord of the Raven, bear witness to our attacks.
L ay here by our brothers,
A nd may they heed the call of Valhalla.

C allous may seem some
A s they fall to the gods' welcome,
L ost warriors they are to your embrace.
L ay here be our brothers,
S ouls that heed the call of Valhalla.

Kai Wonfor (13)
The King John School, Thundersley

Unsupported

Right now she sits at school, exhausted
She wished at home she was supported.
On the floor, empty bottles, too many to count
"Why can't Mum see this is a dangerous amount?"

Every night putting her two young siblings to sleep
Promises for a better life she hopes she can keep.
Then the washing, the cleaning, the homework and weeping
But all she wants is to be calmly sleeping.

In her head, she knows this is not right
When every conversation ends in a fight.
Right now she sits at home, exhausted
She wishes at school she was supported.

Anaïs Buzer (14)
The King John School, Thundersley

Sunny Days

Stop.
Stop my time,
Stop my life.
Pause my never-ending beginning.
Over and over again I see them fly away.
Dissipate into my imaginary image.
Those I love,
Those I see will never last forever
She was my sun
My longing for life,
My missing cohesion.
Scribbling throughout the sky a message.
At least, I hope.
I hope to see her once more, at a later time, for I have lived.
My working days,
My childhood plays
My mother, my father
My loving praise.
Here by me, I stand alone
Just one person wishing to see a glimpse of hope.

Edward Tarbard (14)
The King John School, Thundersley

Tick-Tock, You The Observer

A silent watcher
I mark the rhythm of life with my hands,
As I see the bright sky,
I witness the joys and sorrows that happen that day.

Tick-tock, I go throughout the day,
As the dawn shines, I remind them,
Curious and observant, I feel the hours go by,
Every second of every day.

I desire to perceive,
To sense,
To savour,
But my desires will not be fulfilled.

As I just go tick-tock, as the hours pass by;
As I see the bright sky,
I witness the joys and sorrows that happen that day,
Because there is nothing I can say.

Daniel Cesonis (12)
The King John School, Thundersley

Higher Than Sky, Earth And Sun

Sky high, I am higher.
Void of darkness, not what I desire.
When I look into boundless space.
Something looks back with an ecstatic face.

I do believe it is from the human race,
On a planet so far away.
I've been discovered, I am so gleeful.
Soon I remember I am alone,
This meeting can't change the tone.

So high, out of reach,
Thrashing my deepest of dreams.
Angels are hearing me weep
Rectifying my dreams,
I am no longer whole

Hiatus of life,
Intertwining with me
Get me,
Home please.

Felix Gilbert (13)
The King John School, Thundersley

Seasons

Winter:
Stormy and bitterly cold
That's how it goes
Hard concrete with sleet
I can barely feel my feet

Spring:
I must play and sing
To see the beauty of the spring
I must prance and dance
To get one last glance

Summer:
Now that it's warm
There is not one storm
Finally the time of year for ice cream
So long it felt like a dream

Autumn:
Now it's cold and windy
You can have a nice warm mint tea
The air is crispy and cool
Now I'm the one who's stuck in school.

John Righa (12)
The King John School, Thundersley

Nature Is The Best

N ature is beautiful
A bird is chirping in the midnight air
T he best thing about nature is the trees
U nless there are no flowers, I will always love nature
R oses are the best flowers in the woods
E ndless walking paths are the best
S quirrels walking and running all around the woods

B eautiful flowers blooming on the ground
E ndless line of flowers is amazing
S ometimes I see people walking their dogs
T hough I love home, the woods are my happy place.

Emma Lodge (11)
The King John School, Thundersley

Hero At The Back!

I am a goalkeeper; the hero at the back.
My job is to stop goals from any attack.
This game has only minutes left
And for me, it's been quiet and dead.
But I must stay focused and remain calm in my head.
As quick as a flash, the ball is kicked far down the right wing.
The crowd suddenly erupts and starts to sing.
A low shot has been driven low from the right.
Like a salmon, I dive with no fear or fright.
I catch the ball clean in my hands.
The ref blows the final whistle
And the supporters cheer my name in the stands.

Roman Smale (12)
The King John School, Thundersley

A Day In My Life

I walked through the crowded hallway, my heart rattling in my ribcage,
From the amount of weird looks I got, I knew I needed to make a change.
Walking into school every day knowing something's gonna happen is tough,
And being bullied is an additional point, I've really had enough.
I felt like an animal in a zoo, trapped, unable to escape,
Being held hostage, made fun of, my mouth covered in tape.
I began to continue walking, steadying myself with every step,
So that's a day in my life for you, bullied constantly, yep.

Daisy Stock (11)
The King John School, Thundersley

War's Victims

War is brutal
War is cruel
There are no limitations
There are no rules
Men, young and old
On the fields 'til they are cold
As planes soar in the midnight sky
Children small and tall begin to cry
There are no lights in the London streets
Because of the Grim Reaper, they fear to meet
Thousands dying every day
As children are now being sent away
A station full of mothers beginning to cry
They do not want their children to die
The war has ended, finally
But bodies lay cold for eternity.

Poppy Abbott (11)
The King John School, Thundersley

My Dog's Secret Life

I have a secret, no one else should know,
It's a secret even my parents don't know.
I have a life outside of my home,
One where I can be alone.
I fight crime,
But just hope I have enough time.
My secret life is dangerous,
Only so I don't have to hear anyone say, "Don't be dangerous."
I'm a good dog and good dogs never die,
I stay, my secret life is more than a hobby.
It's to protect; I am very adept at it.
That's my secret life, I strive to get better and better.

Ryden Smith (13)
The King John School, Thundersley

Forever Home

I was 8 weeks old
I wasn't wanted
I had no fur
I didn't know what love was
I was left outside the vets

I had my first cuddle
I had lots of attention
I had fresh water
I had my first proper meal
I had a nice warm bath

She was a nice lady
She gave me cuddles
She showed me love
She made me feel wanted
She took me home

I have a family
I have a name
I have black, shiny fur
I know what love is
I have a forever home.

Maisy-Jai Roberts (11)
The King John School, Thundersley

The Soldier

As the sound of guns fills my head,
I freeze as if the land has taken me hostage.
Sirens wail in the distance,
Like the devil laughing at my presence.

The wind howled like a wolf,
Picking off its prey, one by one.
Soldiers perish at my feet,
Falling like a discarded waste.

The screams they shout are silent,
Though dealing to the ear.
I lay motionless,
As the black void corrupts my vision.

And as the sun sets its final ray,
So does my heart.

Isaac Williams (11)
The King John School, Thundersley

Through The Eyes Of Gypsy Rose Blanchard

In a world of shadows, I once dwelled,
A captive bird in a tale untold,
A life of secrets, a web of lies,
Yearning for freedom beneath the skies,
With a mother's love, or so it seemed,
But behind closed doors,
A nightmare gleamed,
Bound to a wheelchair, my legs so weak,
But my spirit soared, ready to speak,
In the depths of darkness, I found my light,
Unveiling the truth, ready to fight,
No longer a victim, but a survivor,
Breaking the chains revived the light.

Keira Livemore (12)
The King John School, Thundersley

Rucking Into The Battlefield

Fifteen positions, eighty minutes on the front line
A war that's fought on a muddy field
They'll give their last breath to ensure victory is sealed.
Rucking and scrummaging we push through the field.

We start in our own territory
By kicking the ball to our so-called enemies
But after the barbaric eighty minutes
Enemies turn into frenemies.

The once-distant memory
Of having a victory is now sealed
Laughing and cheering as we run
Through the field.

Oliver Plumb (14)
The King John School, Thundersley

The Wire

Through the wire see the fire
See the torture of a young man's future
Young and old they don't care
Kill them all to be fair.

Through the wire see the soldiers
Abusing them like plain old boulders
Send them to the showers
Didn't know they'd end up powdered
In a pile of ashes.

In Auschwitz Birkenau see the views
See them try to flee
Only to be shot dead like a flea.

Through the wire nothing left
Just a desolate emptiness.

Evan Holbrook (13)
The King John School, Thundersley

Why Would You Do That?

Oh... right, what: I didn't sign up for life?
I didn't agree to be heartened or changed.
I thought life was happy, a way to find yourself
No, it is a way to be dragged through pain!
No one really cares
We're all losers, we are all the same
We're told we are doing well
But so is everyone else
We pass a test and so does everyone else
We get a job and so does everyone else
We are all born to die...
Eventually.

Zara Futcher (12)
The King John School, Thundersley

My Older Brother, Rodrick

My older brother, Rodrick
Hits me with a stick
I tell my mum but he calls me a snitch
He hit me so much that I got a stitch

He's always like that
The guy threatens with a bat
With his hat that conceals his bald head
I think he's the family brat

He keeps messing with me
I can't stand it
He's like a bee that never goes away
How would you like it if you're messed with a bit?

Feranmi Fagbohunka (12)
The King John School, Thundersley

The Colour Blue To The Blind

The fresh morning waves crashing at the sand,
The deep breath of summer air,
The ice-cold glass of water clinking,
Blue to the blind.

The cold shower after being at the beach,
The first jump into the pool on holiday,
The sound of flip-flops and laughter,
Blue to the blind.

The feeling of a clear mindset,
The feeling of a fresh start,
The feeling of cleanliness,
The colour blue to the blind.

Hannah Walkom (13)
The King John School, Thundersley

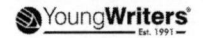

Friendship

F riendship is key
R eminds us that we're not alone
I know that they're not there for me
E ven through the tough times
N ice people in your life
D oesn't make you think twice
S aving you through obstacles
H elping you find your way back home
I love my friends
P lease allow them to stay forever.

Amber Longman (12)
The King John School, Thundersley

Starvation And Hunger

Our eyes as sharp as our teeth
Which is digging inside of animals beneath,
As we search for our main course, through the rough snow
We start to starve, which makes us atrocious
We are reticent through the night
As our pack grows stronger and tight
The deer are near, we move swiftly
Behind them we strike, drag them to our own
We leave not a footprint or scent.

George Otton (12)
The King John School, Thundersley

The Monster Under The Bed

B ehind every bedroom door
R esting under every bed
A brave monster is waiting for quiet
V ictorious and venturous
E very story he listens to
N o one senses that he is there
E ven parents do not believe in the brave monster
S piders and cobwebs are his best friends
S ilent at last, he drifts off to sleep.

Henry Pearch (12)
The King John School, Thundersley

What It Feels Like

Once you feel it,
You will never need to be told,
The love stops the feeling,
Of growing old.

You couldn't bear to ask yourself,
To look for another,
Love is what you need,
Find it in each other.

It's something that can't be beaten,
You won't ever leave it,
It won't be undone,
And it will never be defeated.

Mia Bentley (14)
The King John School, Thundersley

I Am A Mountain

I am a mountain high up in the sky,
High enough to see the beautiful birds fly by,

I am a mountain high above the trees,
High enough to feel the cold bitter breeze,

I am a mountain with one of the most snowy tops,
I watch it carefully as the snow slowly drops,

I am a mountain towering high,
High enough to see the clear, blue, starry sky.

Eden Pearson-Watts (12)
The King John School, Thundersley

Cat's Eyes

After I woke up, after a long, exhausting dream,
I realised I was hungry as could be.
I searched round all the floors of the house,
Looking for a human to feed me!

After a thorough search of the house,
I found a boy, watching noise come out of the telly.
I climbed on his lap and gave him a slap,
And went back to sleep with a full, fat belly.

Leonard Raymond (13)
The King John School, Thundersley

How It Feels To Be Me...

A lways concerned with what people think and
N ever feeling like I am enough
e **X** ercise helps to ease the tensions when
I am overthinking every word you say
E mbarrassed when I break down and cry
T ired from all the pressure I feel
Y ou'll only understand my fear when you step into my shoes one day.

Holly James (12)
The King John School, Thundersley

Fun Fish

Down in the deep
Some fishes will weep
As the desire to swim up
But cannot due to the cuts
On their tails from jellyfish
But at least they're not smelly fish
Some fish try to wish
Others love the clownfish's funny dance
The fish love it and stare in a trance.
Some fishes can bend
Now we are at the end.

Elliot Arthurton (11)
The King John School, Thundersley

Echoes Of Adolesence

Teenage shadows, a weary soul,
Navigating a world, feeling less whole.
Estranged from joy, a heart in strife,
A teenager dances with disdain for life.

Storms within, emotions in disarray,
Yearning for dawn, but dusk holds sway.
Yet, within the dark, a glimmer may appear,
Hope whispers softly, dispelling teenage fear.

William Tutton (14)
The King John School, Thundersley

Once There Was A Dream

Once there was a dream that everyone would be free.
Once there was a dream that we could all have tea.
Once there was a dream a dream.
Once there was a dream that life was equal

Once there was a dream

Once there was a dream that there was no discrimination.
Once there was a dream.
A beautiful dream.

Aaron Eniola (13)
The King John School, Thundersley

Tidal Taker

My golden blanket spans across,
Warming things that I have lost.
My teal body brushes the surface,
Frothing up, returning adventures.

However, for all that I could keep,
It seems to all escape from me.
The ships, bodies, history too,
There's nothing I can't take,
Even from you.

Ellis Lyons (13)
The King John School, Thundersley

My Dog

Where's my ball?
I want to play.
It's the best part of my day.
I love to run and be free.
I love it when my human plays with me.

I run so fast which is so much fun.
My human throws the ball and I catch it and run.
I love my life I love to play.
It's the best part of my day.

Lucy Hayden (12)
The King John School, Thundersley

Skeleton And The Knight

S ilent in the night
K eeping out of sight
E asily hiding from the knight
L eaving the sight at midnight
E ver slipping away like a kite
T hat knight was in for a fright
O ver the moon hiding away
N ever to be found again.

Ava Sussex-Barnes (12)
The King John School, Thundersley

Family

Families are big, some are small,
Some are open and loud
Others are quiet and frail,
Not all perfect, so don't be surprised
If one starts cracking like walls in the night.
Though we may fight
Things stay the same
Because we are family
And nothing shall change.

Violet Siggers (12)
The King John School, Thundersley

My Amazing Dog

In the dark,
In the park,
My dog comes out (to play)
I hear the barks,
His tail sparks,
I hope this sound will stay!

His tail wags,
The squirrel lags,
Off goes my speedy dog!

Tobey Clowes (12)
The King John School, Thundersley

Messi's Magic

Messi is the best footballer of all mankind.
But nobody really knows what goes on in his genius mind.
He is unbelievable and nobody can stop him.
That's why all football fans truly love him.

Kasey Curtis (12)
The King John School, Thundersley

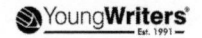

Let Me Go

Let me fly
Across the sky
To my special place
In Heaven where I belong
Not in Hell to me
Go and fly to my special place
In Heaven to watch over
Me and my grandkid.

Alfie Burroughs (11)
The King John School, Thundersley

YOUNG WRITERS INFORMATION

We hope you have enjoyed reading this book – and that you will continue to in the coming years.

If you're a young writer who enjoys reading and creative writing, or the parent of an enthusiastic poet or story writer, do visit our website www.youngwriters.co.uk. Here you will find free competitions, workshops and games, as well as recommended reads, a poetry glossary and our blog. There's lots to keep budding writers motivated to write!

If you would like to order further copies of this book, or any of our other titles, then please give us a call or order via your online account.

Young Writers
Remus House
Coltsfoot Drive
Peterborough
PE2 9BF
(01733) 890066
info@youngwriters.co.uk

Join in the conversation!
Tips, news, giveaways and much more!

- YoungWritersUK
- YoungWritersCW
- youngwriterscw
- youngwriterscw